Into the World of the Dead

Astonishing Adventures in the Underworld

Michael Boughn

Annick Press
Toronto 💀 New York 💀 Vancouver

Annick Press Ltd.
All rights reserved. No part of this work covered by the copyrights hereon may be reproduced or used in any form or by any means – graphic, electronic, or mechanical – without the prior written permission of the publisher.

We acknowledge the support of the Canada Council for the Arts, the Ontario Arts Council, and the Government of Canada through the Book Publishing Industry Development Program (BPIDP) for our publishing activities.

Cataloging in Publication

Boughn, Michael
    Into the world of the dead : astonishing adventures in the underworld / by Michael Boughn.

Includes bibliographical references and index.
ISBN-13: 978-1-55037-959-4 (bound)
ISBN-10: 1-55037-959-3 (bound)
ISBN-13: 978-1-55037-958-7 (pbk.)
ISBN-10: 1-55037-958-5 (pbk.)

    1. Death—Mythology—Juvenile literature. I. Title.

BL504.B66 2006   j202'.3   C2006-900353-X

The text was typeset in Coolman ITC and Brown.

Distributed in Canada by: Published in the U.S.A. by Annick Press (U.S.) Ltd.
Firefly Books Ltd.   Distributed in the U.S.A. by:
66 Leek Crescent   Firefly Books (U.S.) Inc.
Richmond Hill, ON   P.O. Box 1338
L4B 1H1   Ellicott Station
                             Buffalo, NY 14205

Printed in China.

Visit us at: www.annickpress.com

For Jack Clarke,
point man on the journey
—M.B.

Contents

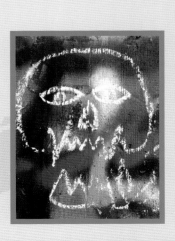

Underworlds

This 16th-century woodcut of the Jaws of Hell is from a book called Livre de la Deablerie.

Mention the underworld to people today, and most will assume you're talking about gangsters. Since about 1900, the term *underworld* has been used increasingly to mean criminals and their illegal activities. Before that time, the underworld was better known for three-headed dogs, sharp-taloned demons, boiling lakes, and sometimes even eternal youth and peace.

Every culture in the world has stories about places that exist beyond the earth we can see around us. Often these legendary places are beneath our feet, literally worlds under us. Just as often, they are worlds of the dead. Some of the earliest human records—pictures painted on cave walls many thousands of years ago—show magicians or priests traveling to these underworlds. Stories of such travels—to speak with the dead, to complete a quest, to bring back a loved one—were told by generations of storytellers, often for thousands of years before they were written down. Today many different versions of these remarkable tales exist. Each story you read here is one particular account chosen from dozens of possible alternatives.

Stories can hold the core beliefs of a culture, which is why so many of these stories are part of sacred traditions. In fact, at one time or another, all of the tales in this book were held to be sacred by someone. Some of them still are. Things have changed, though, and today, in a world dominated by science and technology, few people believe in a literal, physical underworld. Even so, these stories, with their frightening settings, fascinating characters, and marvelous adventures, continue to strike a chord and sometimes terrify us still.

So, as you go into the world of the dead what can you expect to find? Be prepared to witness heroes pitting their courage and wits against the greatest of foes. After all, our deepest fears are represented in these forbidden realms, often in the form of ferocious beasts and demons. A trip to the underworld is the ultimate test of bravery and cunning. The only challenge greater than venturing into the world of the dead is finding your way back out again.

Bon voyage!

John Singer Sargent painted this mural of Astarte, who is also known as Ishtar and Inanna, in the Boston Public Library.

CHAPTER 1

Heaven or Hell?

Hell, Gehenna, and Jahannam

In most people's imaginations, and in portrayals of the underworld, the underworld is deeply connected with sin and punishment. Many stories of dark realms focus on the bad things that happen to you there if you act with cruelty and injustice during your life on earth. Some cultures believed the underworld had various levels, though, almost like a sprawling old mansion full of count-less rooms on different floors. In underworlds such as this, the lower levels were hellish, but the upper levels were heavenly, places where you got to spend eternity in peace.

This 16th-century miniature painting from Spain shows the Christian aerial heaven ruling over the under-world hell.

Judaism, Christianity, and Islam are some-times referred to as Abrahamic religions, because each claims Abraham as a founding prophet. Perhaps not surprisingly, all three faiths share a vision of the underworld as a place where sinners are made to pay for their sins.

Christianity has the most elaborate ideas about the underworld, which is known as Hell. There are various versions of the Christian Hell, but for 2000 years it has generally been portrayed, often in minute detail, as the site of never-ending torment and pain. It is a place of burning, sulfurous lakes, intense, oven-like heat, and eternal darkness, even amidst the flames. For Christians, the underworld is strictly a place where God punishes sinners, who weep and gnash their teeth in never-ending torment. Paradise, or Heaven, is located above the earth in a celestial realm.

For Jews, the underworld is a place of punishment they call Gehenna. It's named after an old dump in a valley outside Jerusalem. History books tell us the dump stank terribly and perpetual fires burned there, which may be why its name was adopted. But as bad as Gehenna was, at least no one had to stay there forever. Jews, unlike Christians, felt that twelve months was long enough to purge dead people of their sins. After that, they could move on to a better place.

Jewish rabbinical literature also refers to an underworld called Sheol, which is strictly neither a place of punishment for

sins nor a place of reward for virtue, but a combination of both. According to the rabbis, Sheol is divided into four areas: one for sinners who profited from their sins on earth; one for sinners who paid to some degree during their lives for their sins; one for the righteous, true and faithful believers; and one for martyrs, people who died for their faith. Sinners suffered various degrees of punishment, the worst being the loss of all hope of resurrection. The righteous dwelt in bliss, an underworld heaven.

The Muslim underworld is called Jahannam, a word derived from the Hebrew word Gehenna. There are seven gates to Jahannam: Jahannam, Laza, Hutameh, Sa'ir, Saqar, Jahim, and Hawiyah. Each of the gates is for a group of non-believers. Atham is a valley of melted brass around the mountain, Sa`ud, the mountain of punishment at the centre of Jahannam. There, the skin of sinners is burned off their bodies and then replaced so that it can be burned off again and again. If they try to escape, they are pierced with iron hooks, which drag them back to the fire. But like the Jewish people, Muslims believe this is only a temporary situation: a sinner with even a small seed of faith in his or her heart will eventually be released from Jahannam.

Hades, the ancient Greek underworld, was much like Sheol, with its own complex geography. As long as you had some money buried with you when you died, you could pay off Charon, the ferryman, to get you over the river. On the other side, Cerberus, a ferocious three-headed guard dog, made sure only the dead proceeded any further. From there, you had to present yourself to Minos, Aeacus, and Rhadamanthus, all sons of the god Zeus, who had been appointed judges of the dead. The three judges would weigh your virtues against your sins and assign you a destination—either Tartarus, for the wicked and unjust, or the Elysium Fields, for the heroic and virtuous.

The Elysium Fields were an underworld heaven where the shades of the dead dwelt in bliss for eternity. In Tartarus, the dead received excruciating punishment—also for eternity. Tantalus, for instance, who had killed his son, Pelops, was placed in a pool of water with fruit dangling over his head. Whenever he was hungry or thirsty, and attempted to eat or drink, the water and the fruit withdrew to a point just beyond his reach. It's from Tantalus's torment that we get the English word *tantalize.*

Tantalus, Sisyphus, and Ixion were all kings whom Zeus, king of the Greek gods, condemned to eternal tortures in Hades, the Greek underworld.

The Sumerians of ancient Mesopotamia called their underworld Ganzir. Ganzir was ruled by the queen of the dead, Ereshkigal, who lived in a palace of lapis lazuli. But Ereshkigal's luxurious way of life was not extended to her subjects. Rather than punishment or reward, what the dead found when they arrived in Ganzir was nothing at all. They wandered naked for eternity, with nothing to drink and only dust to eat. There was no salvation, no rehabilitation, no rebirth. Ending up in Ganzir was not seen as a punishment, because everyone went there when they died, regardless of how they had lived on earth. It was simply destiny. No wonder the famous king and hero Gilgamesh traveled to the ends of the earth (and the otherworld) seeking immortality. With an underworld like that waiting for you, who wouldn't?

Ganzir

Some scholars think this plaque, made between 1800 and 1750 BCE, represents Ereshkigal, queen of the Sumerian underworld.

In Japanese Buddhism, Jigoku is the lowest level of existence, a hellish part of the underworld with regions of both fire and ice, where souls are purified before they are allowed to move on to a higher plane. The Buddhist underworld has 21 levels, some of which, such as Svarga, are heavens. The god Yama, who is the lord of the underworld for Hindus and Buddhists alike, rules over them all.

This Japanese painting is from the 13th-century Scrolls of the Hells.

Ancient Egyptians believed that the souls of the dead would be judged by Osiris in the underworld. Although the geography is a bit confusing, one version has the soul arriving first in Amenti, the place of the setting sun. Using the spells, magic charms, formulas, and passwords in *The Egyptian Book of the Dead*, the soul would then travel in the solar boat to Tuat where Osiris would decide its fate. If its heart was found to be pure, it would pass on to Aaru, where it would dwell forever in peace and harmony.

Tuat

The Egyptian Book of the Dead, *from which this page is taken, was buried with the mummified dead in order to help them find their way through the underworld.*

Mictlan

The Aztecs, who ruled Mexico before the Europeans came, believed in an underworld with nine different levels. These levels allowed like souls to congregate after death: the souls of warriors gathered together in a certain place, for example, as did women who had died in childbirth. The ninth and lowest level of the Aztec underworld was called Mictlin, and that is where most people went when they died. The journey to Mictlin was said to be long and dangerous, taking four years, but once you had arrived, you existed peacefully for eternity.

Xibalba

The Mayans, who lived around the same time as the Aztecs but further south, also believed in an underworld with nine levels. The underworld was called Xibalba and the ninth level was called Mitnal. Mitnal was cold, dark, and dank, a place of eternal punishment for those who had sinned against the gods and their fellow humans.

Naraka

Like the Aztecs and the Mayans, the Hindus have many levels in their underworld, Naraka. These are places of punishment, though, where the dead undergo such terrible torments as being boiled in oil. Naraka is ruled by Yama, the lord of death, whose job was to assign souls to their proper punishment: the trials most suited to the sins a person had committed while alive. As in Gehenna, however, such punishment is primarily for rehabilitation. After a suitable period of suffering, each soul is thought purified and ready to be reborn.

Like underworlds, otherworlds exist beyond what we can see. Otherworlds aren't under the earth, though. Sometimes they are thought to be beyond the edge of the world. Sometimes they are thought of as places where the dead dwell. Some people believed them to be the home of supernatural creatures like fairies and elves. It wasn't quite as hard to get into the otherworld as it was the underworld; usually, all you needed was a fairy guide.

The Irish tell many stories of people who journeyed to the otherworld. Bran mac Febal was a great warrior, who was put to sleep by magical music and awoke holding a silver branch. A fairy led him to the otherworld, where he discovered a land of eternal youth and beauty. In another Irish story, Connla, the son of Conn Cétchathach, convinced a beautiful fairy woman to take him to the otherworld, which he refused to leave, preferring eternal youth over his father's throne. In parts of Africa, the otherworld was a kind a mirror world to ours, a reflection that existed at the bottom of a lake. And sometimes it was an island far off in the sea. Some people think that St. Brendan, an Irish saint who died in 577 CE, sailed in a leather boat to the other world where he saw many wonders —including a land of spirits in the form of birds.

Otherworlds

The English poet and artist, William Blake, painted this picture of fairies in the otherworld for Shakespeare's A Midsummer Night's Dream.

CHAPTER 2

The Way In

In the ancient world, there were many ways to get into the underworld. Some of them even appeared on maps. The Mayans thought the entrance to Xibalba was through the mouth of a huge feathered serpent. Other stories tell of underworld travelers entering through a lake, the mouth of a cave, or a certain door in a temple. Usually you had to search for the entrance to the underworld, but sometimes you simply fell into a hole, or the earth opened up, and the next thing you knew, you were there.

Persephone

Persephone (her Roman name was Proserpine, though she was also called Kore) was the daughter of Demeter, the ancient Greek goddess of the earth, and Zeus, the king of the gods. Zeus' brother, Hades, king of the underworld, fell in love with Persephone. With Zeus' permission, but unknown to Demeter, Hades plotted to kidnap Persephone and make her the queen of his dark realm.

One day, as Persephone wandered through the fields with her nymphs—spirits associated with natural features such as rivers, forests, and the sea—she noticed a path of wildflowers stretching across a distant meadow. She had never seen anything quite so exquisite, and she began to follow the path, picking the flowers as she strolled. Before long, she left behind all of her companions.

Suddenly a rumbling rose from the ground at Persephone's feet. It sounded like a runaway team of horses coming closer and closer, though there were no horses in sight. Persephone turned to flee, but it was too late. The rumbling became a deafening roar, and she shrank back in horror as the earth split open, exposing a gaping black hole. Out of it rode Hades in a four-horse chariot. Before Persephone could cry for help, he snatched her up, turned his horses, and plunged back into the earth. The hole closed behind them without leaving a trace.

The chariot flew down into the darkness, and Persephone could see nothing until they came to Hades's realm. He lived in a magnificent palace in the Elysium Fields, a part of the underworld with its own sun and stars. The chariot stopped there. When

Persephone realized that she was being held by her father's brother, she began to scream. How dare he kidnap her, a daughter of Zeus? She threatened Hades, she pleaded with him, but nothing could move him to return her to the earth. In grief and fear, Persephone sank into a deep silence, refusing to eat or to speak.

None of the nymphs had seen what happened, and no one on earth knew what had become of Persephone. Demeter was beside herself with worry. She roamed the world seeking news of her daughter's whereabouts, getting no answers until Hecate, another goddess, took pity on her and revealed the

truth. Filled with fury, Demeter demanded that Zeus return her daughter.

"It is a fine marriage," Zeus said, trying to placate the earth goddess. "My brother rules over a third of the world, and Persephone is now his queen."

"You and Hades stole my daughter, and she must be returned," Demeter insisted. But Zeus would not budge. Demeter's anger grew and grew, until finally she retreated into the temple at Eleusis and refused to allow the earth to bring forth food.

The grain shriveled, and no new grain sprang up in its place. Without grain to eat, cattle and sheep began to die. With neither bread nor meat to eat,

This illustration showing the abduction of Persephone (known to the Romans as Proserpine) is from an early 20th-century edition of Nathaniel Hawthorne's Tanglewood Tales, *in which Hawthorne retold many classical Greek myths.*

people began to die off, too. There was no one left to make sacrifices to the gods, and Zeus missed receiving these sacrifices. Relenting, he summoned Persephone from Hades (the place itself bore the underworld king's name) to Eleusis. Once word came that Hades must relinquish his bride, he desperately sought a way to bind her to him.

"Before you go," he begged Persephone slyly, "at least honor me by partaking of these pomegranate seeds."

Persephone was so overjoyed at the thought of rejoining her mother that she took a few seeds and ate them.

The reunion between mother and daughter was ecstatic. After the two of them had hugged and kissed, however, Demeter thought to ask Persephone a very important question: "You didn't eat anything in the underworld, did you?" To her mother's horror, Persephone admitted to eating the pomegranate seeds. In all innocence, she had broken one of the cardinal rules about going to the underworld: never eat anything while you're there. If you do, you must stay in the underworld forever.

Once again, a dispute broke out about what would happen to Persephone. Having consumed the seeds, she was inescapably bound to the underworld. However Demeter argued that Persephone should be allowed to remain above ground for at least part of the year because she had eaten only three.

And so a deal was struck among the gods: Persephone would live with her mother on earth for part of each year, then descend through the dark, ominous portal to reign as the queen of the dead. This arrangement, the ancient Greeks believed, explained why plants grow on the earth for only part of the year. When Demeter was mourning for her daughter, the world was barren.

In this illustration from Hawthorne's Tanglewood Tales, *Persephone (Proserpine) is reunited with her mother. The god standing behind them is Hermes (also known as Quicksilver because of his association with the planet Mercury) whose job was to conduct the souls of the dead into, or in this case out of, the underworld.*

Doorways to Hell

While the underworld may be no more than a story to some people, to others it is right around the corner. A web site in the United Kingdom posts over a hundred photos, not unlike these, of entrances to hell in the United Kingdom that the site creators claim have been authenticated by investigators and scientists. Are there any entrances in your neighborhood?

The Zuni Spirit Wife

The Zuni people of what is now the southwestern United States tell the story of a man whose young wife had died. The man loved her so much he decided he could not let her go on to the underworld without him.

"Release me," her spirit cried out to him. "Only the dead can make this journey."

"No," he told her. "I cannot live without you."

Finally, she gave in and helped him devise a plan.

"It is a long and dangerous journey," she told him, "and during the day I will be invisible to you. You must find a red feather and tie it in my hair so that when you no longer can see me, you will still be able to follow the feather."

This the young man did, and as the sun rose over the mountains and deserts they must cross, he watched his wife fade away, leaving only the feather in view. He followed the dancing feather out of the village, through the fields and into the wilderness, always heading west toward the land of the setting sun. Each day he would follow the red feather until he was too tired to walk any more. Then he would sleep. His spirit wife came to him in his dreams.

They traveled along paths no wider than a thumb and over steep, bottomless chasms. One day, the young man watched as the feather floated into the air over a deep canyon.

"Stop," he called, but his spirit wife couldn't hear him. The feather landed on the other side. He tried to climb down the canyon but soon found himself clinging to its sheer walls with nothing more than a crack to hold on to. "Surely," he thought, "I, too, will die now."

But just when it seemed he was doomed, a small squirrel appeared at his head.

"Hold on, foolish young man," the squirrel said to him, "and I will help you." The animal took a seed from its mouth and planted it in the crack, chanting magic words over it. The seed began to sprout and grow at a miraculous rate. Before long the plant had spanned the canyon, and the young man pulled himself onto it and crawled across. On the other side, he found the feather waiting for him.

After many more days, the man and his spirit wife came to an enormous dark lake. At the bottom of the lake lay the underworld, but the young man knew he could not follow his wife into the water. In despair, he watched the red feather disappear beneath the waves.

As the young man wept, he was approached by an owl spirit. The owl blew some medicine from a magic bag into the young man's face. The young man fell into a deep sleep, and owl men carried him to a hill overlooking the lake. They laid him under some trees, then swooped down to the land beneath the lake where they found the young woman's spirit and brought her back to the land of the living.

The young man and his wife were thrilled to be reunited. The spirits warned them, however, that the man must not touch his wife until they were safely home. They traveled for many days together. Then, within sight of their home, the man forgot the rule: he joyfully embraced his wife. She faded away before him, and he never saw her again.

This woodcut by the 19th-century French artist, Gustave Doré, shows Lucifer and his friends falling into Hell after being defeated in their war against Jehovah.

The great Italian poet Dante Alighieri, in a long poem called *The Inferno*, wrote of his descent to the depths of Hell, the Christian version of the underworld. Along the way, he encountered lovers trapped in a damp whirlwind, unable to touch each other, and sinners who were buried in putrid soil, torn apart over and over again by the three-headed dog Cerberus, immersed in a river of boiling blood, or encased in ice—all for eternity, of course. The illustration above depicts the Mouth of Hell as Dante described it.

Dante's Inferno

CHAPTER 3

Why Go?

Journeys to the underworld are invariably portrayed as difficult and dangerous. The place itself is always terrifying. So why on earth (so to speak) would anyone want to go? Some people ventured into the underworld in the hopes of bringing back a great prize. Others sought important information from the dead. Sometimes a person was kidnapped and taken to the underworld. The all-time most popular reason for risking all by going to the underworld, though, is to bring back a loved one from the dead. Almost every culture has a tale about that.

These skulls are carved into the ruins of the Mayan temples at Chichen Itza in Mexico.

Kubaiko

Kubaiko was a young Tartar girl. Her people were nomadic and lived on the Sayan Steppe in what is now Mongolia. The Tartars, also called Mongols, were fabulous horse riders and fierce warriors. Under the leadership of the great warrior Genghis Khan, they created an empire that stretched all the way from the Pacific to the Black Sea in the 1200s.

When Kubaiko's brother died, so the story goes, his head was stolen by evil demons who hid their booty deep in the underworld. Knowing that her brother's spirit would never rest until his head had been recovered, Kubaiko vowed to bring it back to earth.

Her vow was not an easy one to keep. Finding her way to the underworld was hard enough, but once Kubaiko got to the entrance, the journey became even worse. It took every ounce of courage she possessed to step onto the path that led into the bowels of the earth, but she did so, stopping only to light a torch. The way down was steep and dark. Spiders and snakes scurried and slithered before her in the gloom. At first, the roots of the grasses that grew above brushed Kubaiko's face. But more terrifying were the shadows that moved just beyond the light of her flickering torch. These were the hulking, misshapen demons that were all the more frightening for their vague resemblance to humans. They screeched at Kubaiko, threatening to tear her to pieces and eat her once her light was gone.

Just as her torch was sputtering, Kubaiko entered a large chamber with an immense throne in the middle. All around, on the walls of the cavern, jewels sparkled in rock, lit by some fluorescent radiance. Off to the side, seven red horns poked up out of the ground.

"What mortal dares come before me?" a deep voice boomed. The earth shook as the Irle Khan stepped from behind his throne and glared down at

This mask of the Mongolian Irle Khan, Tshoijoo, is used in dances that celebrate the battles of the gods against their enemies.

I will offer you a chance to win back your brother's life. Do you see these seven horns that stick up through the rocky floor?"

"I do," Kubaiko said.

"They belong to a red ram, which is buried beneath the floor. If you can grab those horns and pull the ram up through, then I will restore your brother to you."

Well, if the heart of the Irle Khan was made of iron, so was his brain. In fact, the ram buried beneath his floor was the sun. The seven horns were the seven planets that crown the sun's glory. And the sun, as everyone knows, rises whether or not someone pulls it up through the earth.

Kubaiko leapt to her task with the energy and heart that had brought her to the underworld in the first place. She grabbed the horns and began to wrestle with them. Her muscles bulged as she tugged and pulled on the huge horns. Even as she did so, the sun began its daily journey. Kubaiko hid her surprise, pretending to struggle with the great ram as it rose slowly but surely out of the floor of night and into the morning sky.

The Irle Khan was as good as his word. Once he saw the red ram rise, he restored Kubaiko's brother to life and sent them both home, whole and well. Kubaiko was overjoyed at the rebirth of her beloved brother, and her people greeted her as a great hero.

Kubaiko. Kubaiko stared back in horror at his monstrous face. His eyes bulged, white fangs protruded from his grotesque mouth, and horns thrust up out of his head alongside a crown of skulls.

It was all Kubaiko could do not to run back to earth. But she steeled herself, straightened her back, and looked straight into the Irle Kahn's terrible eyes.

"I am Kubaiko," she said, "and I have come for my brother's head."

The Irle Kahn had never seen such courage in a mortal. His heart was made of iron, as it must be, for everyone who has lost a loved one pleads for them to come back; the rulers of the underworld must say no, or no one would ever die. The bravery of this small girl moved Irle Kahn though. Ponderously, he considered how to reward her for reaching his kingdom. He couldn't make it too easy for her. After all, he was Death, and this was his realm. So he decided to present her with a challenge.

"Kubaiko," the Irle Khan said, "you have ventured far and overcome many obstacles. Therefore,

Odin's spear was named Gungir. It never missed its target.
The wolves, Freki and Geri, went with him everywhere.

Odin

Odin was the powerful leader of the Norse gods known as the Aesir. The gods made their home in Asgard, which was connected to Middle Earth by a rainbow bridge. Below Middle Earth, was Niflheim, the underworld, which was ruled by Hel, the underworld's queen.

Odin's son was Baldur, the god of light and the most beautiful of all the gods. When Baldur grew troubled by dark, disturbing dreams, Odin decided to travel to the underworld to ask a dead prophetess what the nightmares meant. Odin saddled Sleipner, his eight-legged horse, left Asgard, crossed the rainbow bridge, called Bifrost, and descended into the frigid depths of Niflheim. Odin rode swiftly past Garm, the snarling hellhound whose chest was covered with dried blood and whose red eyes burned like fire, and came to the hall of dead ruled by Hel. He made his way to the mound where the prophetess was buried and chanted a rune spell to raise her from the dead. When her tomb opened and she appeared before him, Odin demanded to know the meaning of Baldur's dream. The prophetess told him that Baldur would die by his brother's hand and there was nothing Odin could do to stop it. The leader of the gods rode back to Asgard with her wicked laughter pealing in his ears.

Orpheus and Eurydice

Orpheus was the most accomplished musician in the ancient Greek world. Whenever he played, the animals gathered around him to listen, and even the trees and stones danced to his music. Orpheus met and married a woman—or nymph—named Eurydice. Their love for each another was deep and strong. Then one day, while out with her companions, Eurydice was pursued by a minor god who desired her for his wife. As she fled from him, she stepped on a poisonous snake. Its bite was fatal, and Eurydice's spirit departed for the underworld.

Orpheus was wracked with grief. His music became so sad that even the gods were driven to weep. He eventually decided that he couldn't live without Eurydice and must go into the underworld to find her. Playing his pipes as he walked, Orpheus descended deeper and deeper until he stood face to face with Hades, the god of the underworld.

Like other gods of the underworld, Hades was famous for being hard-hearted. But even he couldn't resist the beauty of Orpheus's music. Tears came to his eyes, and he cried out for Orpheus to stop. Hades agreed to allow Eurydice to return, but only on one condition: Orpheus could neither look at his wife nor speak to her until they were back on earth.

Orpheus had made it almost to the top of the climb when he was seized with worry. He could no longer hear Eurydice's footsteps behind him. Had she had gotten lost or separated? Had Hades lied to them? The more Orpheus thought about it, the more worried he became, until he could not restrain himself: he glanced behind him. Eurydice looked back in shock as she began to fade, and her spirit was carried away by Hermes, the god who guides all souls to the underworld.

This painting of Orpheus appealing to Hades and Persephone for the life of Eurydice was painted by Jan Bruegel the Elder, a Dutch artist, in 1594.

Inanna

Jesus

Inanna is portrayed here as the goddess of battle. This image is taken from a 2000-year-old Sumerian cylinder seal.

Early Christians told the story of how Jesus descended into the underworld after his crucifixion and before his resurrection. He pounded on the gates of Hell, striking fear into the hearts of Hell's demons. Once inside, he rescued all the innocents who were trapped there, souls who had died before Jesus was born. Adam and Eve, the first man and woman, were among them. Satan was not happy to have his realm invaded, and some versions of the story claim that he and Jesus wrestled until Jesus finally subdued him. The incident came to be known as the Harrowing of Hell.

Inanna was the great Sumerian goddess of love, fertility, and war. She ruled the surface of the earth, but lured by the desire for power, or perhaps mere curiosity, she journeyed to the underworld. Inanna's own sister, Ereshkigal, ruled there. As Inanna passed through the seven gates of the underworld, Ereshkigal tricked Inanna into giving up all her protective amulets and clothing and fixed her with an "eye of death" instead.

As an ancient poem says, *"Inanna was / turned into a corpse, / A piece of rotting meat, / And was hung from a hook on the wall."*

After three days and three nights, Enki, the father-god of civilization and of Inanna herself, sent two magical creatures created from his fingernail parings to bring her back to life. The creatures tricked Ereshkigal into giving up Inanna, but before she could return to life on the earth, Inanna had to pick someone to take her place in the underworld. She chose Dumuzi, her own shepherd-husband whom she decided had not mourned her properly while she was dead.

This miniature picture of Jesus walking over Satan as he enters Hell is an illustration in a medieval Dutch book.

Of the several hundred warriors who sailed to the otherworld with Arthur, only seven returned to tell the tale.

Arthur

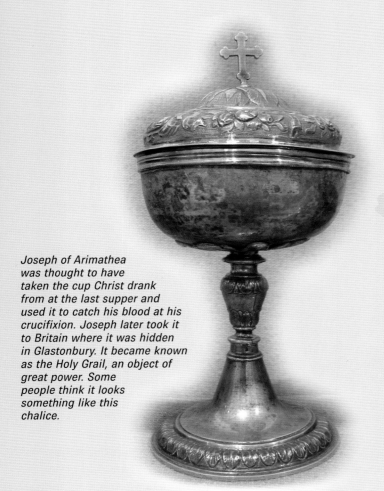

Joseph of Arimathea was thought to have taken the cup Christ drank from at the last supper and used it to catch his blood at his crucifixion. Joseph later took it to Britain where it was hidden in Glastonbury. It became known as the Holy Grail, an object of great power. Some people think it looks something like this chalice.

According to the poet Taliesin, the Welsh hero Arthur, who became King Arthur and built Camelot and the Round Table, traveled beyond this world to the end of the earth. He and a ship full of his fellow warriors sailed into the otherworld, Annwfn, seeking a magical cauldron that belonged to Arawn, the ruler of Annwfn. The cauldron, which had pearls around its rim and was heated by the breath of nine maidens, was said to have the power to magically heal wounds and to bring good fortune to the one who possessed it, if he were truly brave. The cauldron was held in a fort known as Caer Prydryvan. Arthur and his crew faced 6000 fairy warriors there, fought a bloody battle, and were defeated. They were driven back to earth without the prize they had set out to capture. Some scholars think this cauldron gave rise to the Arthurian legend of the quest for the Holy Grail.

CHAPTER 4

Who Went?

Both mortals and supernatural beings have ventured into the underworld. Some underworld travelers were already great heroes when they set out. Some were ordinary people who became heroes because of their journey. Various gods and goddesses made the trip for reasons of their own. But one thing is certain: you can't descend into the underworld without facing a test of your courage.

The Hero Twins

The twin Mayan gods One-Hunter and Seven-Hunter were renowned for their skills as ball players. During one game, they made such noise that they disturbed the lords of the underworld. These lords—who included One-Death, Pus Master, Bone Scepter, and Bloody Claws—invited the twins down to Xibalba. (When the lords of death invited you for a visit, you couldn't really say no.) The lords tricked their two guests into undergoing a series of tests, then killed them.

The god One-Hunter had left behind two sons—the twins Hunahpu and Xbalanque. These young twins were also excellent ball players, and after some time their ball-playing too disturbed the lords of Xibalba. The lords were not happy.

"Get them down here," thundered One-Death. "We'll deal with them as we dealt with their father and uncle."

Bone Scepter wrote an invitation and had an owl deliver it to the young twins.

"You must be very careful," their worried mother told the young twins. Hunahpu and Xbalanque listened respectfully to her warning. They knew it was their destiny to confront the lords of death, however, so they prepared themselves for their journey.

The passage to Xibalba was fraught with peril. The young twins made their way through thorny calabash trees and over raging rivers full of spikes, blood, and pus. When they came to a crossroads, they followed a black road that took them to the throne room of the lords of the underworld.

Pus-Master, oozing pus, rose to greet them.

"Welcome to Xibalba," he said. "We have arranged a few trials for you during your stay."

Hunahpu answered bravely. "We're ready," he said.

The trials the lords of the underworld had set up involved spending six nights in six different houses. At the first house, Hunahpu and Xbalanque peered inside. It was the House of Knives, they realized. Razor-sharp steel edges glinted everywhere, waiting hungrily for something to cut. The twins gathered up some dead animals and threw them into the house. The knives were happy eating the animals, and they left the twins alone for the night.

The next night the dark lords led them to the Cold House, in which the twins were meant to freeze to death. But they sealed up the house with leaves and mud to make it warm, and once again escaped death. The following night, at Jaguar

The sacred ball game in early Meso-America was a bit like lacrosse, except that the losers were often sacrificed to the gods.

House, the twins collected all the bones they could find and fed these to the jaguars, again thwarting the evil lords.

In the Bat House, their luck ran out when a bat bit off Hunahpu's head. It turned into a ball, which the lords gleefully bore off to use in the game the next day. The twins had many friends among the animals, however, and they helped by making a fake head for Hunahpu out of a pumpkin.

Hunahpu wore the pumpkin head to the big ball game. During a break, Rabbit switched the pumpkin for Hunahpu's real head. When the game resumed, Xbalanque kicked the pumpkin so hard it smashed into a thousand pieces, spreading its seeds everywhere.

However, the contest wasn't over yet. The lords still hoped to kill the twins, this time by burning them up in a fire. Because they could see into the future, the twins knew they had to die. They also knew that the lords of Xibalba would ask the prophet Xulu what to do with their bones. They plotted with Xulu to trick the lords one final time.

"Can you convince the lords to grind up our bones and scatter them in the river?" they asked the old prophet.

"Of course," he replied. "Don't worry."

Their plan in place, the twins leapt into the fire. The prophet went to see the lords.

"If you really want to be rid of those pesky twins," he told them, "you had best grind up their bones and spread them in the four directions."

The lords of the underworld followed the prophet's advice, and it worked. The twins came back to life, first as catfish, then as a pair of singers whose music was so powerful it moved One-Death and Seven-Death to sacrifice themselves in the fire. When the other lords realized what had happened, they surrendered to the twins.

Rather than kill the remaining lords, the twins gave them a set of rules. The lords were no longer allowed to eat humans, and they now ruled over only the souls of people who had been violent or guilty of something really bad on earth. This new system established order in the world.

For their last feat, the twins attempted to bring their father back to life. Although they were unsuccessful, they did rise up into the sky to become the sun and the moon and became known as the Hero Twins.

Naciketas

Yama is one of the oldest known beings in the world, having first appeared in the Hindu Vedas, first written down around 1500 BCE. In one form or another, as Yama, Ymir, Emma, or Yima he has been worshipped all over Europe and Asia.

The story of Naciketas is told in the *Katha Upanishad*, the sacred Hindu book. Naciketas was the son of a poor but pious man who was trying to detach himself from worldly things by giving them away. But the man couldn't quite bring himself to let go of the good stuff; instead, he got rid of some old cows and some broken pottery. Upset with his father's hypocrisy, Naciketas demanded sarcastically, "Father, to whom will you give me?" His father tried to ignore him, but Naciketas persisted. He kept repeating his question until finally, in anger, his father shouted, "I give you to Yama." Naciketas's father had consigned him to the Hindu god of death.

Although Naciketas didn't feel ready to die, he remembered that everything mortal must die some-time, and he went obediently to Yama's palace. When he got there, he discovered that Yama was away. Naciketas settled down to wait. The first day, no one attended to him. He sat and sat, patiently waiting for Yama to return. No one brought him food on the second day, either, or offered him anything to drink. Again Naciketas sat and sat, patiently waiting for Yama's return. On the third day, he was ignored again, and although he continued to wait patiently,

he did begin to think that the god of death was very rude to leave a visitor so long unattended.

On the fourth day, the lord of death rode up on his fierce black buffalo. Because Naciketas was a virtuous person, Yama appeared to him as a friendly figure with four arms, lotus-shaped eyes, and a wonderful smile. (Had Naciketas been a sinner, he would have seen Yama as a monster, roaring and breathing smoke.) When Yama realized that Naciketas had waited for three days without food or drink, he was deeply embarrassed.

"I will make it up to you," Yama told Naciketas, "by granting you three wishes."

Naciketas thought long and hard. He didn't want to make foolish choices, as so often happens in fairy stories. "For my first boon," he respectfully told the great lord of death, "I would like to be guaranteed safe passage back to my father."

Yama smiled, recognizing the young man's wisdom. "Of course," he said. "And for your second?"

This was more difficult. Others might wish for wealth or fame, but these things, Naciketas knew, were ephemeral—they might last for a few days only and then be gone. Finally he hit upon it. "For my

The ancient Greek hero Odysseus was on his long journey home from the Trojan War. Along the way Odysseus angered the sea god, Poseidon, by blinding Poseidon's one-eyed son, a Cyclops named Polyphemus. In retaliation, Poseidon kept blowing Odysseus's ship off course. Circe, an enchantress, advised Odysseus that he must ask the dead prophet Teiresias how to get home to Ithaca and to his wife and son. So Odysseus and his crew set sail for the underworld. They sailed until they came to the river Oceanus, which circled the earth, where they found the spot where the rivers Cocytus, Phlegethon, and Acheron met at the end of the world. There they dug a pit and filled it with blood from a white sheep and a black sheep. The shades of the dead came swarming up from Hades to drink the blood and talk with the mortals. Teiresias's ghost told Odysseus what dangers lay ahead of him and what he must do to get home.

This picture of Odysseus summoning the spirits from the underworld is from an early-20th-century translation of Homer's Odyssey.

second boon," he said, "I desire to understand how the immortal ones are freed from sorrow and the fear of old age."

Yama willingly shared this knowledge with Naciketas, demonstrating for him how a human might transcend the circle of birth and death and reach higher realms of existence.

Feeling emboldened, Naciketas then made the greatest wish of all—he asked to know about life after the great passing on.

Yama shook his head. "The knowledge you seek is not for mortals," he said. "I cannot grant this wish."

But Naciketas would not to be swayed. He repeated his request until Yama relented and revealed to him the atman, the supreme self, which in the Hindu tradition enables a person to see beyond the veil of the world to the truth of existence. With that vision, Naciketas achieved enlightenment. He was never again subject to the passions or to death, even after he returned to earth and his father's house.

Dominic Padrini, an 18th-century Italian painter, painted this picture of Herakles dragging Cerberus out of the underworld.

Herakles

The mighty Greek hero Herakles (also called Hercules) killed his own children after being driven mad by the vengeful goddess Hera. According to some ancient sources, King Eurystheus gave Herakles twelve tasks to atone for his terrible crime. These tasks—so difficult and dangerous they were thought to be impossible—were known as the Twelve Labors of Herakles. If he achieved them, he would attain immortality. For his final and most perilous labor, Herakles descended into the underworld to bring back Cerberus, the vicious three-headed watchdog. After wrestling Cerberus into submission, Herakles dragged the hell-hound from Hades to King Eurystheus, who then commanded him to take the dog back again. If Cerberus looks familiar to modern readers in this illustration, it may be because he resembles Fluffy, the three-headed pup from *Harry Potter and the Philosopher's Stone*. Fluffy stood guard at the entrance to the underground vault where Harry confronted Voldemort for the first time.

Oisín, the son of the Irish chief Fionn mac Cumhaill, was a famed warrior and poet. He went to Tir na nOg, the Celtic otherworld, after falling in love with golden-haired Niamh, daughter of Tir na nOg's king. Oisín stayed for three years, but he became so homesick that he begged to be able to return to his companions. Reluctantly, Niamh sent Oisín home on her magical white horse, warning him that he must not touch the soil of Ireland. When he accidentally fell to the ground, Oisín instantly aged by 300 years, for every year in the otherworld is equal to 100 years on earth.

Stephen Reid painted these two pictures of Oisín for a book called The High Deeds of Finn and other Bardic Romances of Ancient Ireland, *published in 1909.*

Oisín

The Young Hopi Man

This photograph of the Hopi Snake Dance was taken by Edward S. Curtis in 1905.

The Hopi of northeastern Arizona tell the story of a young man who doubted that the sacrifices made by his people actually went to the gods. He decided that traveling to the Lower Place was the only way to find out for sure, although everyone warned him against it. The route the young man followed was arduous, and several gods in human form tried to frighten him into turning back. But the young man persevered. With the help of Deer-Kachina-Cloud, a spirit who took pity on him, the man got as far into the underworld as Snake Village. There he found a bride, and the two of them began the long journey back to his home. By the time they arrived, the man's wife was pregnant. She waited outside his village, warning him not to touch anyone until he returned to her. But one of the young man's old lovers embraced him before he could stop her. Weeping, his bride returned to her people, leaving the young man with their son. The Hopi Snake Dance commemorates the man who went to the underworld and the snake woman he married.

CHAPTER 5

Getting There

Getting to the underworld was definitely no easy matter. Simply finding the entrance was often a challenge, and travelers were almost always plagued by hideous and dangerous creatures along the way. Since the underworld was generally reserved for the dead or for spirits of one sort or another, making the trip while you were still alive was very risky. For this reason, many stories of the underworld focus on the arduous business of getting there.

This picture from an illuminated Renaissance manuscript shows Aeneas holding the golden bough in the underworld as he talks to one of the spirits he met there.

Aeneas

Aeneas was a warrior who fought for the Trojans during the ten years the ancient Greeks laid siege to Troy. When the walls of Troy were breached, thanks to the trick horse the Greeks had built, Aeneas escaped carrying his father on his back. The gods told Aeneas that he would found a new nation greater than Troy, but that he must first sail across the Mediterranean to the land we know today as Italy.

After many adventures and the death of his beloved father, Aeneas landed. The first thing Aeneas did was visit the cave of the 700-year-old sibyl, a prophet through whom the god Apollo was reputed to speak. The sibyl seemed to confirm that Aeneas would be successful in founding a new nation, but Aeneas asked for more.

"I want to travel to Hades to speak with my father," he told the sibyl. " I understand that your cave is an entrance to the underworld. How can I get in?"

The sibyl laughed. "Anyone can get in to Hades," she told Aeneas. "The problem is getting back out again. If you want to return to the world of sunlight, you must first go into the forest and find the tree

This is a map of the underworld as Aeneas encountered it. The rivers Acheron, Phlegethon, Cocytus, and Styx flow into the Stygian Marsh. The dead can only cross into the underworld if they have the money to pay the ferryman, Charon. On the other side, past Cerberus, the road forks. One way leads to Tartarus and eternal punishment. The other leads to the Elysium Fields and eternal bliss.

You can still visit the sibyl's cave at Cumae, where this photo was taken.

that bears golden boughs. Break one off and bring it back as a gift to Persephone, the queen of the dead."

With the help of Aphrodite, his goddess mother, Aeneas found the golden bough, and the sibyl led him to the entrance to Hades. There they sacrificed sheep and poured out libations to the gods, calling for the goddess Hecate, queen of the night, to open the way for them. The earth began to shake, and a sulfurous stench filled the air. Dogs howled. The sibyl instructed Aeneas to

The Dutch painter, Jan Bruegel the Elder, painted this scene of Aeneas and the sibyl in the underworld in 1600.

draw his sword, and together they plunged into the dark hole that Hecate revealed to them.

Many grotesque, terrifying creatures lined the way down: centaurs, half-human, half-horse; snake-haired gorgons; filthy winged harpies. Aeneas's heart raced as he reached for his sword, but the sibyl held him back. The two of them continued until they came to the Acheron, one of the four rivers of the underworld. There they saw Charon, the ferryman who took newly arrived souls across the marsh.

"Wait," Charon roared as they moved toward his boat. He pointed at the blade protruding from Aeneas's cloak. "He's not dead. He can't cross."

Aeneas reached again for his sword, but the sibyl restrained him.

"Yes," she said to Charon, "what you say is true. But we come bearing this gift for Persephone." She pulled the golden bough from the folds of her cloak. "Would you deny your queen this prize?"

Seeing the glint of the golden bough, Charon agreed to transport them. They were no sooner across than they were confronted by Cerberus, the beast that guarded the entrance to Hades. Aeneas drew back in alarm. But from under her robes the sibyl produced a cake of honey and oats laced with a strong sedative. The giant dog devoured it and soon fell asleep.

The path before Aeneas and the sibyl wound through the gloom to the distant palace of Hades. At a fork in the road, Aeneas was hailed by shadowy figures in battle dress. These were the shades of the many friends and enemies he had known during the long siege of Troy. The sibyl urged Aeneas onwards, warning him that their time was running out.

The sky became brighter and brighter in the light of the underworld sun until the palace emerged before them in all its magnificence. Carefully, Aeneas laid the golden bough on the steps leading up to it. From there, he and the sibyl traveled to the Elysium Fields. Here Aeneas found and joyfully embraced his father, Anchises, and the two of them spoke about the mysteries of life and death. All too soon, the sibyl signaled that they must leave. Anchises accompanied them to the Ivory Gate of sleep and sent them through it back to the world of the living. Aeneas carried with him knowledge that no other mortal had ever possessed.

Charon

Charon, the ferryman of Hades, was the son of Erebus, the primordial god of darkness, and of Nyx, the embodiment of night. He was a ragged and grumpy old man, perhaps a minor god, although no one knows for sure. Charon was adamant about one thing: if the newly dead had not been buried with coins (two obols) under their tongue, he would not ferry them into the underworld. The poor souls would then have to wander the banks of the river for a hundred years.

Anansi

The Ashanti people of west Africa have many stories about the trickster god, Anansi, or Spider. In one story, Anansi and his son, Ananute, were out hunting when Ananute found a big, juicy palm nut. Before he could eat it, the nut slipped out of his hands and fell into what looked like a rat hole. Ananute dove through the hole and found himself in a kind of underworld, where he was greeted by three spirits who had not washed since the creation of the world. The spirits gave Ananute some yams, telling him to cook the peels and throw away the meat. For obeying, he was rewarded with an endless supply of good yams back on earth. But when the jealous Anansi jumped down the hole, he laughed at the spirits for their dirty appearance. He kept the yams they gave him and threw away the peels, making the magic vegetables go rotten.

This picture of Charon and Cerberus is from a book called The Pantheon, *published in 1735.*

Hiku and Kawelu

The Hawaiians tell the story of Hiku (also called Hiku-i-ka-nahele: Hiku of the forest). He met Kawelu on the shore of the ocean when she found and hid an arrow he had shot and was searching for. He stayed with her for six days without being offered food. When he finally left angry, Kawelu chased after him, but it was too late. With Hiku gone, Kawelu died of a broken heart.

When Hiku simmered down and came looking for Kawelu, he was distraught to discover that she had died. He vowed to go to Milu, the underworld, to bring back her spirit. Following his mother's instructions, he and his friends made a strong rope by weaving vines together. They paddled out to the point where sky and sea meet the horizon and found the spot Hiku's mother had referred to as the great drop. This was the way to the underworld.

Before he could get into Milu, however, Hiku had to disguise himself as a corpse. He rubbed his body all over with rancid coconut oil so that he would smell as if he were decaying. He and his friends then tossed the vine rope over the great drop and Hiku slid down it, carrying with him a coconut shell cut in half.

Hiku quickly realized that Milu was not unlike the world of the living. Everywhere around him the spirits were playing games with each other, participating in sports and doing hula dancing. Shrewdly, Hiku invited them to play a new game that involved swinging on his rope. Many spirits, including Kawelu's, flocked to the vine. Hiku swung the rope back and forth until he had tempted Kawelu's spirit to grab hold and go for a ride. When her spirit did, he pulled it up to the surface of the world. Kawelu's spirit tried to escape by turning into a butterfly, but Hiku captured the butterfly between two coconut shells and took it home. After making a small incision in the big toe of Kawelu's body, Hiku pushed her spirit in, bringing Kawelu back to life. The two lovers embraced and soon after were married.

Gilgamesh

Gilgamesh, the Sumerian hero, journeyed to the underworld and beyond after the death of his dearest companion. His search for the secret of immortality took him across a vast desert. At the tunnel leading through Mount Mashu, he was challenged by two giant scorpions, whom he talked into letting him pass. The trip through the mountain took days and days in absolute darkness. Gilgamesh emerged in the beautiful garden of the gods where the trees bore jewels and precious stones on their limbs. He then had to sail across the Waters of Death, which would kill anyone who touched them. On the far shore, in Dilmun, the Land Where the Sun Rises, he finally found Utnapishtim, the only man ever granted eternal life by the gods. Utnapishtim agreed to make Gilgamesh immortal if he could stay awake for six days and seven nights; unfortunately Gilgamesh fell asleep. Utnapishtim also helped him find a magical plant that would renew his youth, but a snake stole the plant from Gilgamesh on the trip home.

This modern sculpture of Gilgamesh is based on a 3000-year-old original and shows the ancient king with his attributes, a lion and a snake.

CHAPTER 6

Who's in Charge

The ruler of the underworld has been imagined in many different ways. Most cultures saw the underworld's boss as a fearsome figure with immense supernatural powers, but exactly who you'd encounter at your destination depended on the beliefs of your people. Some rulers took on different guises according to the situation, too: for example, Yama, the lord of both the Buddhist and the Hindu underworlds, could appear wrathful to the cruel and selfish or kind to those who had led good lives.

Early Christians had many grotesque images of Satan.

Satan

Satan, the ruler of the Christian underworld, was not always evil, nor was he always known as Satan. In the beginning his name was Lucifer, "the Morning Star." When God, or Jehovah, created the world, separating dark from light, water from earth, he also created many beings—angels—made of pure light to share his creation with him. Of all the angels, Lucifer's light shone brightest. His six wings shimmered with a heavenly brilliance, and he sat at God's left hand, where God could look down upon his glory and delight in it.

"Aren't I a wonder," Lucifer said to himself, "more splendid than anything else in creation." And then came the fatal thought, "If I am so perfect, so marvelous, why must I subject myself to the authority of another? Who is greater than I?"

Lucifer looked around the heavens and saw that only one sat higher than he: God himself. Even the Archangel Michael sat below Lucifer. But rather than be happy at his remarkable status, Lucifer was angry. "Why should God sit above me?" he thought. "We ought at least to sit side by side. And if he were fair, surely he would allow me to sit on the throne once in a while."

Gustave Doré made this woodcut of Satan brooding over a frozen hell to illustrate Dante's Inferno.

Lucifer's anger grew along with his pride. When God decided to create Adam, the first man, Lucifer's jealousy threw him into a rage.

"How dare he create this beast out of mud and clay and expect me to worship it?" he fumed. "Soon he'll be putting Adam in my chair."

Deep in his heart, Lucifer turned on his creator, and he began to plot against him. His chance came when Jehovah left his throne to check on Adam. Seizing the moment, Lucifer ascended the throne and summoned all the angels to hear what he had to say. As he sat at Heaven's highest point, looking out over the masses of assembled angels, he thrilled at the sight. "This is my due," he thought, "to be worshipped and obeyed."

"Why," Lucifer began, addressing the radiance before him, "why must we, the greatest beings in creation, subject ourselves to the unjust authority of some tyrant? Are we not individuals? Don't we have rights?"

Some of the angels began to cheer.

"We have free will," Lucifer shouted. "We have the right to choose our leader. Choose me, and I will lead you to new heights. We will restore Heaven to its former moral purity."

No one knew exactly what that meant, but fully a third of the angels (133 306 668 of them, according to the 15th-century Bishop of Tusculum, who concerned himself with such matters) were ready for a little excitement. They lined up behind Lucifer with the intention of setting up an alternative kingdom in Heaven.

Those who didn't agree with Lucifer rallied to the call of the Archangel Michael, who declared war on the revolutionaries. Gathering the angelic hordes about him, Michael launched an attack on Lucifer's army. Back and forth the battle waged all day long. Though outnumbered two to one, Lucifer's forces managed to hold their own—until Jehovah returned.

Once God saw what had happened in his absence,

Contemporary popular culture tends to treat the devil more lightly.

Ah Puch

he was enraged. With one mighty blow, he struck Lucifer from the throne and sent him and his minions hurtling through space. Down and down they fell, picking up speed as they went. With each moment, their light dimmed and their beauty faded, until their skin had turned dark and leathery, their wings had shriveled, and their faces had become twisted and hideous. These former angels hit the earth with such terrific force that the planet split open and swallowed them. Down they fell until they reached the fiery bowels of the planet, and there they landed in a vast, burning, sulfurous lake.

And so Lucifer became Satan, which means "adversary" or "accuser" in Hebrew. From his new home in Hell, Satan rallied his demonic forces to go forth into the world and spread evil wherever they could. He swore never-ending hatred toward God and all his works, and he began by corrupting Adam and Eve, tempting them into the same disobedience that had him thrown out of Heaven.

Muslims have a similar story about an angel named Iblis. Like Lucifer, Iblis was first among God's creations. Iblis's act of disobedience, however, was a bit different. When Allah demanded that Iblis pay homage to Adam, Iblis refused, because he felt it was insulting for an angelic creature to bow down to a creature made of mud. After his fall, Iblis became known as Shaytan.

Ah Puch likes to hang around the houses of the sick and injured.

Ah Puch ruled the lowest and worst of the nine levels of the Mayan underworld, Xibalba. He was thought to haunt the houses of the sick and dying, looking for victims to drag down to Mitnal. For one of his favorite costumes, he would dress in a putrefying human corpse with an owl's head, adding a few bells for adornment.

Osiris

The ancient Egyptian god, Osiris, was married to his sister, Isis. Their parents were the ancient Ones, gods who had created the heavens and earth out of nothing. Osiris and Isis ruled together over Egypt, teaching humans how to read and write, how to raise crops, and how to build functional and elegant structures. All was well, except that their brother, Set, was jealous of Osiris. He longed to take Osiris's place on the throne of Egypt and make Isis his own wife.

Set was devious, and he worked out a plan with 72 other conspirators to kill Osiris. He invited his brother to a feast. Midway through the celebration, Set stood up and addressed the crowd.

"I have prepared a gift," he told the group, "a gorgeous coffin that I will give to whomever among you can fit into it."

A coffin was a marvelous gift in ancient Egypt, and indeed, this casket was the most beautiful anyone in the crowd had ever seen. One after another, the guests tried it on for size, and one after another they were disappointed. Finally Set turned to his brother and said, "Dear brother, won't you try?"

Somewhat reluctantly, Osiris agreed. What he didn't know was that Set had had the casket made specially to fit him and that it was also fitted with a magical lock. Once Osiris had lain down in the coffin, Set slammed it shut and locked it. He and his followers threw the coffin into the Nile River, where Osiris drowned.

Isis spent many years searching for the coffin before locating it in a massive tree that had been cut down for use as a pillar in the palace of the King of Phoenicia. She returned with her husband's body to Egypt. When Set

Ancient Egyptians painted this picture of Osiris and Isis on a papyrus scroll now in the British Museum in London.

found out, he attacked Osiris again, this time cutting his brother's body into 13 pieces and scattering them about the world.

Isis gathered the scattered parts of her husband's body. With the help of Anubis, the guardian of the dead, she then mummified Osiris, an act meant to preserve the body from putrefaction and prepare it for resurrection. With the proper magical burial rites, Isis resurrected Osiris, who then returned to the underworld. He became the great judge of the dead, sending just souls to paradise and condemning the unjust to oblivion.

Mictlantecuhtli and Mictecacihuatl

Mictlin, the lowest level of the Aztec underworld, was ruled by Mictlantecuhtli and and his wife, Mictecacihuatl. They were gruesome creatures, skeletons with crowns of skulls, protruding teeth, and organs hanging from their rib cages. Mictlantecuhtli was often represented wearing a necklace made of human eyeballs. It was said that the pair dined sumptuously on meals of beetles, beetle gas, pus, and decaying human hands and feet.

Although this statue of Mictlantecuhtli is a bit scary, he really wasn't a bad guy for a ruler of the underworld.

Vacub-Caquix

Vacub-Caquix, a giant bird demon, cut off the head of the Hero Twins' father and hung it in a tree.

In Xibalba, the Mayan underworld, a giant bird monster was the ruling demon. His name was Vacub-Caquix or Seven-Macaw. Vacub-Caquix was very arrogant, and he set himself up as the sun god, carrying a false sun in his beak and claiming to be the lord of creation. The Hero Twins were angered by his presumption and decided to kill him. Hunahpu shot a blow-gun dart at the bird monster but only managed to hit him in the jaw. In a rage, Vacub-Caquix ripped off Hunahpu's arm. After it healed, the Hero Twins tricked Vacub-Caquix into having his teeth replaced with corn. The monster weakened and died.

CHAPTER 7

Guardians and Monsters

Almost every underworld had monsters guarding the entrances and exits. Sometimes they were to keep the dead in, and sometimes to keep the living out. Some monsters had the sole duty of tormenting those who ended up there. The monsters of the lower realm were terrible in an astonishing variety of ways, but it was common for them to be decked out in death's finery—tatters of rotten flesh, skulls, eyeballs, maggots, and worms. In many instances, the gate-keeper monster was some kind of a dog—and not the kind of pooch you'd want to meet in a dark alley, either.

The English poet William Blake drew this picture of Cerberus for Dante's Inferno.

Bad Dogs

Cerberus, guard dog to the ancient Greek underworld, had a noble lineage for a monster. His father, Typhon, with his hundred heads, lava pouring from all his mouths, and venom squirting from his eyes, was so terrible even the gods fled from him. Typhon had found his perfect match in Cerberus's mother, Echidna, whose lovely head was made hideous by the constant writhing of her snake body. The Greek poet Hesiod described Echidna as *"divine / and iron-hearted, half fair-cheeked / and bright-eyed nymph / and half huge and monstrous snake inside the holy earth, / a snake that strikes swiftly and feeds on living flesh."* Cerberus was the perfect pet for Hades, king of the underworld. The only people ever known to get by him were Orpheus, who charmed Cerberus with his music, and Aeneas and the sybil, who drugged the giant dog.

In the Finnish underworld, Tuonela, the death goddess also kept a pet. The goddess Kalma—who stank of rotting flesh—had Surma, who kept his mouth wide open at all times so that he was ready to rip to shreds any soul who tried to escape.

Cwn Annwn, the red-eyed hell hound of Arawn, the Celtic otherworld lord, also chased down escaping spirits, making sure none got out of Annwfn. Some people thought that the crying of wild geese was actually the baying of the hounds as they pursued the souls of the damned.

This mural from the tomb of Pu Nentwy shows Anubis and other gods at the weighing of the heart of the dead person against a feather.

Anubis and Ammit

In ancient Egypt Anubis, who had the head of a jackal, was worshipped as the god of death. As more and more people began to worship Osiris, however, Anubis's job changed. He became the god who brought newly dead souls before Osiris to have their hearts weighed. The stakes were high: if your heart weighed more on the scales than the feather of Truth, you were judged unworthy of eternal life. That's where Ammit came in. With the head of a crocodile, the body of a leopard, and the hind quarters of a hippopotamus, Ammit embodied not just one but three fierce, man-eating animals. Anubis would throw the hearts of the unworthy to Ammit. She consumed then hungrily, condemning her victims to oblivion.

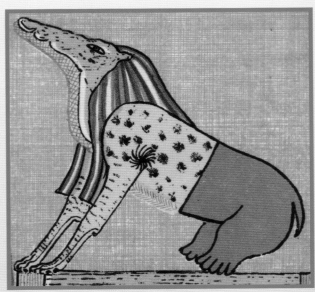

This picture of Ammit is copied from the Papyrus of Ani, an Egyptian text found in Thebes in 1888.

Whiro

The Maori, the aboriginal people in what we now call New Zealand, believed that their well-being on earth was threatened by an underworld monster called Whiro. Whiro was a lizard god who dwelled deep in the bowels of the earth and preyed on humans who hadn't protected themselves with the proper spells and charms. He had an army of demons to help him possess people, spreading disease and pain and misery. The Maori considered Whiro and his demons to be the source of evil in the world, inspiring humans to act violently towards each other, dividing communities, and sowing discord.

Baal

Baal was the chief demon of the Christian underworld, Hell, with 70 legions of lesser demons at his command, each charged with breeding a specific evil. Baal's own specialty was causing idleness among people. He was said to be able to grant invisibility to those humans who invoked him, although damnation was their fate if they failed to control him. Like that of most demons, Baal's appearance was odd, to say the least. He had three heads—a cat, a toad, and a man—perched atop the body and legs of a spider.

Jikininki

Among the most terrifying underworld monsters were the tormented spirits of the dead, which haunted the earth. In Japanese Buddhism, the souls of people whose greed had prevented them from dying peacefully became Jikininki. These creatures were a cross between a zombie and a ghoul but maintained something of their human forms even as their bodies were rotting. They rose up from the underworld to eat the flesh of the newly dead, stealing corpses from graves not only for flesh but for clothing and jewelry.

The Egyptian snake god Neheb-Kau was a kindly guardian of the underworld, and a primeval figure believed to be linked to Ra, the sun god. In the underworld, Neheb-Kau protected and fed the pharoah, and he was responsible for offering food and drink to the "justified dead" as well. Living people prayed to Neheb-Kau to protect them against venomous snake bites.

Neheb-Kau

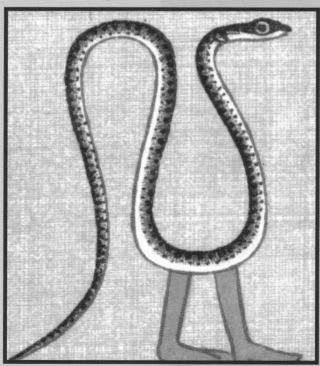

Also from the Papyrus of Ani, this picture of Neheb-Kau is part of the Egyptian Book of the Dead.

Gustave Doré drew these furies, which the ancient Greeks believed tormented people guilty of crimes.

These harpies greeted Aeneas when he entered the underworld.

Harpies and Furies

The harpies and the furies were residents of the Greek underworld. Harpies were bird women resembling vultures. Their claws were made of steel and their foul breath ruined whatever they breathed on. In Dante's *Inferno*, they are depicted as tormenting the souls of those who had committed suicide. They were able to snatch away the souls of the newly dead, as well as those of small children and the weak and sick.

The furies were three sisters who were sometimes portrayed as the goddesses of vengeance. In that role, they punished particularly those who had broken "natural laws" such as murdering a family member. The living feared the furies so much that they referred to them superstitiously as the Eumenides, "the kindly ones."

The Jabberwock

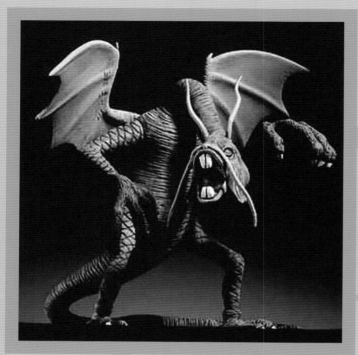

Lewis Carroll wrote a famous nonsense poem about the Jabberwock.

The Jabberwock, with eyes of flame,
Came whiffling through the tulgey wood,
And burbled as it came!

In his book *Alice's Adventures in Wonderland*, Lewis Carroll wrote about a little girl who entered the underworld by falling down a rabbit hole. In a second story, *Through the Looking-Glass*, Alice slips into the otherworld through a mirror. There she hears the story of the Jabberwock, a fabulous monster that lives there.

Ga-Gorib

Heitsi-Eibib, the famous hero of the Khoikhoi people in Africa, battled and defeated the monster Ga-Gorib, who sat by the side of a huge hole in the ground and dared people to strike him with a stone. The stone always flew back at them, knocking them into the hole, and they were never seen again. But Ga-Gorib met his match in Heitsi-Eibib. Instead of throwing the rock, Heitsi-Eibib insulted the demon. They chased each other around the hole until they both fell in. No one knows for sure what happened underground, but when Heitsi-Eibib crawled back up to the earth, he was licking his lips.

Asmodeus

The Christian Hell was full of countless demons who had followed Lucifer during the War in Heaven and were condemned to damnation along with him. Asmodeus, with the heads of a bull, a ram, and a man perched atop the feet of rooster, was the demon who provoked people to adultery and meaningless fads. He was also believed to have invented music, dancing, and theatre.

This ancient Aztec statue of Coatlicue is now in the National Anthropology Museum in Mexico City.

Coatlicue

Coatlicue, whose name means "Serpent Skirt," was the earth goddess of both life and death in Aztec mythology. Coatlicue had a horrible appearance: wearing a skirt of rattlesnakes and a necklace of hearts torn from human victims sacrificed to her. Two snakes wound out of her neck and faced each other. Her hands and feet were sharp claws. Coatlicue's husband, Mixcoatl, was the cloud serpent and god of the chase.

CHAPTER 8

Getting Back

As abodes of the dead, underworlds are meant to house spirits forever. The rulers are extremely hesitant to let any of their subjects out, since that would diminish their kingdoms. But stirring tales are told of those brave travelers who managed to find their way back to the upper world. If you are planning on traveling to the underworld, may your story be one of these.

Kwan-Yin

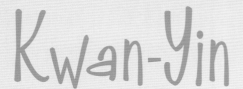

Kwan-Yin was said to have been Miao Shan, the highly accomplished daughter of a king of the Chou dynasty in China, around 1000 BCE. Since she was from such a wealthy, powerful family, Kwan-Yin was offered every luxury. But extravagant clothes and lavish parties meant nothing to Kwan-Yin. She did not so much look down on the fabulous embroidered silk robes; she simply did not care about them. Her family's exquisite gardens were no more precious to her than the weeds by the roadside. Kwan-Yin was not interested in worldly things. Instead, she wanted to spend her life meditating on the mysteries and blessings of creation.

One day Kwan-Yin's father announced, "I have found a husband for you. His family is rich and has many connections in the court. It will be a good union. The marriage will be in the spring."

"But Father," she said, "I don't wish to marry. I want to become a nun."

Her father's fury was quick and violent. "You disobedient wretch," he screamed. "If you want to live in the temple, go."

What her father didn't tell her was that the Buddhist monk in charge of the temple owed him a favor. The king sent the monk a message, instructing him to give Kwan-Yin the dirtiest, smelliest, most awful jobs. "Then let us see if she still desires to be a nun," he finished his letter.

But for Kwan-Yin, dirty jobs and clean jobs were all the same. She continued to be surprised by the beauty she found everywhere. Wherever she went, she sang, and the very stones seemed to quiver with joy. No matter how difficult the monk made her life, she didn't even seem to notice.

This turn of events further infuriated her father. Calling Kwan-Yin home from the temple, the king again demanded that his daughter marry the man he had chosen. Kwan-Yin stood before him, unafraid,

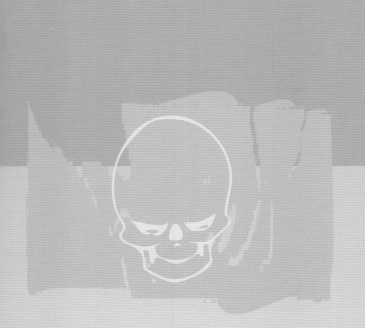

Because Kwan-Yin is so popular, bringing beauty and compassion to people's lives, there are thousands of different images of her.

and gently but firmly refused. Her very gentleness incensed him, and in a blind rage the king summoned a servant to cut off her head. If her father thought this would frighten Kwan-Yin, he was wrong. She neither pleaded for her life nor cowered in fear, but instead stood smiling as if she were sorry for the king.

When the servant learned who his victim would be, he was saddened. Like all who had heard Kwan-Yin sing, he wanted only to go on listening to her. Having some small magical abilities, he secretly worked a spell on his sword. He raised the blade high over Kwan-Yin's neck, but when he brought it down, rather then slice through her innocent flesh, it shattered into a thousand pieces.

Kwan-Yin's father ordered the servant out of his sight and called in a man who had killed for him in the past. He handed the man a pillow and commanded, "Hold this over my daughter's face until she no longer draws a breath."

Without a pause, the man suffocated Kwan-Yin.

One minute Kwan-Yin was in her father's palace, and the next she was riding on the back of a celestial tiger on her way to the underworld. She marveled at the tiger's strength and speed and began to make up a song about it. By the time they arrived in the underworld, she was singing her song. The tiger bowed to her and stayed to listen.

As the sound of Kwan-Yin's singing spread through the underworld, strange things happened. In Jigoku, that part of the underworld where the unjust and cruel are punished for their crimes and purified,

the flames of torment were suddenly extinguished and flowers shot up everywhere.

"What's happening to my kingdom?" demanded Yama, the god of death.

An underling pointed out Kwan-Yin. All the formerly gloomy spirits were now gathered around her, smiling and tapping their feet.

"This won't do," Yama shouted. "Send her back to earth at once."

And so Kwan-Yin suddenly arrived back in the upper world. She had discovered an unlikely way out of the underworld. But to her it didn't matter, because her song went on just as before. She floated in the heart of a lotus flower to an island called Putuo, from which she dispensed compassion, love, and mercy to those who were suffering in the world. When she heard that her father was dying of an illness, she cut flesh from her own arm to be used in a medicine. After she had healed him, her father recognized his error and repented his cruelty. To honor his daughter, he ordered a magnificent statue of her to be made.

Izanagi and Izanami

In Japanese Shinto stories, Izanagi and Izanami were the first couple. They created the island of Japan by thrusting a jeweled spear into the sea. Together, they made all the gods. But when Izanami gave birth to the fire god, she was consumed by flames and perished.

Crippled with grief, Izanagi decided to pursue Izanami's spirit to Yomi, the underworld, and bring her back. He found her there, but it was so dark that he couldn't see her clearly. Izanami told Izanagi he was too late: she had already eaten the food of the underworld and was now bound to stay. But if he would wait for her, she said, she would appeal to the lord of the underworld for special dispensation. Izanagi agreed to wait and not to enter Izanami's room while she was gone.

Izanagi waited a long time, but Izanami didn't come back. When a horrible stench filled the air, he wanted to find its source. Breaking his promise, he followed the smell into a small dark room. He pulled the ornamental comb from his hair, causing it to burn brightly. What he saw horrified him. Before him lay his once-beautiful wife, now a rotting corpse crawling with maggots and worms. Izanami was furious that Izanagi had broken his word and hence seen her in her present state. Enraged, she chased him all the way back to the surface of the earth. Panting with fear and exertion, Izanagi slammed a huge boulder over the entrance to Yomi, forever separating the two worlds.

This modern image of Izanagi and Izanami on the bridge of heaven was painted in 1850 by Utagawa Hiroshiga.

Maruwa

The Wachaga people of Tanzania tell the story of a young girl, Maruwa, who was supposed to guard the family bean plants. Maruwa got thirsty, however, and she went down to the Kiningo pool to get a drink. While she was gone, baboons came and cleaned out the bean plot.

To escape punishment from her father, Maruwa ran back to the pool and jumped in. She sank slowly to the bottom, into a kind of otherworld. Many people were living there, and she stayed with one old woman and a little girl for a long time. The old woman forbade Maruwa from helping the little girl with her chores, but Maruwa felt sorry for the girl and helped her anyway. One day the little girl warned Maruwa that she must leave the otherworld or be trapped there forever.

"Go to the old woman and tell her you are homesick," the girl advised. "But listen carefully: when she asks you whether you want to go home through the manure or through the fire, tell her the manure."

Maruwa did as the girl had told her. The old woman threw her into the manure pile, and before she knew it Maruwa was back in the upper world. She was covered in jewels and ornaments, a reward for having helped the young girl.

The Man Who Loved Death Maker's Daughter

The Mayans told a story of a mortal man who fell in love with Death Maker's lovely daughter. The man followed her to the underworld to try to win her as his bride. He was hiding in Death Maker's kitchen when Death Maker's wife found him. She could see how much the man loved her daughter, and so she took pity on him, hiding him under a blanket of chilies harvested from the earth. Death Maker ate only rotten food—tortillas made from stinking fungi, beans of the larvae of large green flies that swarmed around the dead, and corn paste made from decayed flesh. Because the odor of earth-grown chilies repulsed him, he didn't notice the smell of the human hiding under them. "Don't eat anything," Death Maker's wife told the man, "or you'll never get out of here." But reverse magic proved true as well. The man got some tortillas made from corn grown on the earth and convinced Death Maker's daughter to eat them. Immediately, both of them were expelled from the underworld. Back on earth, they were delighted to marry.

Hatupatu

Hatupatu, the hero of the Maori people, was killed by his brothers out of jealousy while they were all hunting birds. However, Hatupatu came back from the dead and decided to return to his home.

On the way home he was pursued by the birdwoman monster, Kurangaituku. Just as she was about to grab him, Hatupatu shouted a magical incantation and commanded a large boulder to open up. The rock split open, and Hatupatu dove into the ground. In the nick of time, the rock closed behind him. Kurangaituku screeched and clawed at the boulder for a long time. When he could no longer hear her, Hatupatu set off again for home, but Kurangaituku was lying in wait. This time Hatupatu ran to a place where geysers burst through the ground. He was able to dodge through them, but Kurangaituku wasn't; she was carried down into the earth, from which she never emerged again. People say that, if you are in New Zealand near a place called Atiamuri, you can see the boulder that split open and allowed Hatupatu to escape. Kurangaituku's claw marks are still there in the face of the rock.

AOTEAROA
NEW ZEALAND

80c Kurangaituku
Giant bird-woman

The New Zealand postal service created this stamp with the image of Kurangaituku to mark the Year of the Dragon in 2000.

Further Reading

D'aulaire, Ingri. *D'aulaires Book of Greek Myths*. NY: Bantam, 1992.

Echlin, Kim. *Inanna*. Toronto: Groundwood Books, 2003.

Fisher, Leonard Everett. *Gods and Goddesses of the Ancient Norse*. NY: Holiday House, 2001.

Green, John. *Celtic Gods and Heroes*. NY: Dover Publications, 2003.

Krulik, Nancy. *Hades: The Truth at Last*. NY: Hyperion, 1997.

Mollel, Tololwa M. *Ananse's Feast: An Ashanti Tale*. NY: Clarion Books, 1997.

Morley, Jacqueline. *Egyptian Myths*. NY: NTC Publishing Group, 2001.

Philip, Neil. *Eyewitness Mythology*. NY: DK Publishing, 2005.

Philip, Neil. *Mythology of the World*. NY: Kingfisher, 2004.

Sutcliff, Rosemary. *The Wanderings of Odysseus*. NY: Dutton, 2005.

Zeman, Ludmila. *Gilgamesh the King*. Toronto: Tundra Books, 1999.

Selected Sources:

Arnott, Kathleen. *African Myths and Legends*. Oxford: Oxford University Press, 1963.

Bierhorst, John. *The Mythology of Mexico and Central America*. NY: Morrow, 1990.

Cotterell, Arthur. *A Dictionary of World Mythology*. NY: Perigree, 1979.

Crossley-Holland, Kevin. *The Norse Myths.* NY: Pantheon Books, 1980.

Eliot, Alexander. *Myths*. NY: McGraw-Hill, 1976.

Erdoes, Richard and Alfonso Ortiz, eds. *American Indian Myths and Legends*. NY: Pantheon, 1984.

Read, Kay Almere and Jason Gonzalez. *Handbook of Mesoamerican Mythology*, Santa Barbara, CA: ABC-CLIO, 2000.

Leeming, David. *A Dictionary of Asian Mythology*. Oxford: Oxford University Press, 2001.

Morgan, Genevieve and Tom. *The Devil: A Visual Guide to the Demonic, Evil, Scurrilous, and Bad*. San Francisco: Chronicle Books, 1996.

Rolleston, T. W. *Celtic Myths and Legends*. Mineola, NY: Dover Publications, 1990.

Wall, J. Charles. *Devils*. London: Methuen, 1904.

Image Credits:

Cover image background, based on Source: Library and Archives Canada/Roloff Beny collection/PA-199773; **10,** Source: Library and Archives Canada/Roloff Beny collection/PA-199602; **12,** Source: Library and Archives Canada/Roloff Beny collection/DAPDCAP 488347; **31 lower,** Source: Library and Archives Canada/Roloff Beny collection/PA-199567; **48,** Source: Library and Archives Canada/Roloff Beny collection/DAPDCAP 488347. All © Library and Archives Canada. All reproduced with the permission of the Minister of Public Works and Government Services Canada (2005).

Cover image middle, 28, © Christie's Images/CORBIS; **7 lower,** Bettmann/CORBIS; **9 upper,** Burstein Collection/CORBIS; **11,** Bettmann/CORBIS; **19,** © SETBOUN/ CORBIS; **21,** © Arte & Immagini srl/CORBIS; **26,** © Historical Picture Archive/ CORBIS; **30,** © Gianni Dagli Orti/CORBIS; **40,** © Werner Forman/CORBIS; **43 upper,** © Sandro Vannini/CORBIS; **50,** © Peter Harholdt/CORBIS.

1, 42, *Illustrations to the Divine Comedy of Dante* by William Blake. The National Art Collection Funds: London, 1922.

2, *The Devil Turn'd Round-Head* by John Taylor, London, 1642; **3 second,** *La Magie Noire,* Paris: 19th century; **4,** *Libre de la Deablerie,* printed by Michel Le Noir, 1568; **9 lower,** *Book of the Dead;* **47 upper,** Tobit, 3:18. All courtesy *Devils, Demons, Death and Damnation* by Ernst and Johanna Lehner. Dover Pictorial Archive series, Dover Publications, Inc., 1971.

3 top, istockphoto Inc./Clayton Hansen; **third,** istockphoto Inc./Joseph Yap; **bottom,** istockphoto Inc./Dan Brandenburg; **7 upper, 51 lower, back cover image background,** istockphoto Inc./Diane Miller; **15 upper,** istockphoto Inc./Matt Craven; **right,** istockphoto Inc./Alex Mills; **left,** istockphoto Inc./Nicola Wadowski; **16 upper,** istockphoto Inc./Kelly Pollak; **lower,** istockphoto Inc./Julie Deshaies; **18,** istockphoto Inc./Kevin Lafferty; **23 lower,** istockphoto Inc./Bart Parren; **25 lower,** istockphoto Inc./Tobias Gelston; **34 background image,** istockphoto Inc./Nicholas Belton; **middle image,** istockphoto Inc./Justin Griffith; **35 right,** istockphoto Inc./Kevin Tate; **38 left,** istockphoto Inc./Dennis Cox; **51 upper,** istockphoto Inc./Steve Geer; **52 left,** istockphoto Inc./Norman Eder; **52 right,** istockphoto Inc./duckycards.

5, John Singer Sargent. *Boston Public Library Decorations in the Copley Prints.* Boston: Curtis & Cameron, 1902: LC-USZ62-133767; **29 lower,** *The North American Indian,* Edward S. Curtis Collection, 1906: LC-USZ62-113080. All courtesy Library of Congress, Prints & Photographs Division.

6, *Lectionary Lectionarium,* Catholic Church, 16th century; **22 right,** *Dutch Hours;* **47 lower,** William Henry Jackson, Detroit Publishing Co., 1900; Yale Collection of Western Americana. All courtesy Beinecke Rare Book and Manuscript Library, Yale University.

8, © Copyright the Trustees of The British Museum.

13, 14, *A Wonder Book and Tanglewood tales for girls and boys* by Nathaniel Hawthorne. Illustrated by Maxfield Parrish. Duffield and Company, 1910. By permission of the Osborne Collection of Early Children's Books, Toronto Public Library.

17, 45 left, *Cassell's Doré gallery: containing two hundred and fifty beautiful engravings selected from the Doré Bible, Milton, Dante's Inferno, Dante's Purgatorio and....* by Gustave Doré and Edmund Ollier, 19th century; **27,** *Odyssey* by Homer and Henry Bernard Cotterill. Illustrated by Patten Wilson. George G. Happap & Co., 1911; **33 left,** *The Pantheon, representing the fabulous histories of the heathen gods and most illustrious heroes: in a short, plain and familiar method, by way of dialogue* by Andrew Tooke. 13th ed. D. Midwinter, 1735; **37, 45 right,** *The Vision of Hell* by Dante Alighieri. Illustrations by Gustave Doré. Cassell, Petter & Galpin, 1866; **39, 43 lower, 44, back cover third,** *The Papyrus of Ani; A reproduction in facsimile ed, with hieroglyphic transcript, translation and introduction* vol.1 by E. A. Wallis Budge. Philip Lee Warner, 1913. All courtesy Toronto Public Library.

20, 22 left, 35 left, 49, back cover top, Special thanks to Sacred Source/Ancient Images Ancient Wisdom; PO Box 163; Crozet, Virginia 22932; ph.: 800-290-6203; f.: 434-823-7665; spirit@sacredsource.com; www.sacredsource.com.

23 upper, *The Romance of King Arthur and his knights of the round table* by Sir Thomas Malory. Abridged by Alfred W. Pollard. Illustrated by Arthur Rackham. London: Macmillan, 1917.

25 upper, © Justin Kerr; K1209; www.mayavase.com.

29 upper left and right, back cover second, *The High Deeds of Finn and other Bardic Romances of Ancient Ireland* by T. W. Rolleston. Illustrated by Stephen Reid. New York: Thomas Y. Crowell & Company, New York: 1909.

31 upper, 38 right, 41, Art by Joe Weissmann.

32, Erich Lessing/Art Resource, NY

33 right, Art by Stéphane Jorisch.

36, *The Devils* by James Charles Wall. London: Methuen, 1904.

46, back cover bottom, Special thanks to ToyVault Inc.;10053 US HWY 25 South; Corbin, KY 40701; ph.: 606-523-9776; www.toyvault.com.

53, Courtesy New Zealand Post, the producer of this stamp, with special thanks for giving Annick Press permission to reproduce it.

Index